You Can't Eat Flags For Breakfast

YOU CAN'T EAT FLAGS
FOR BREAKFAST

Poets – Politicians – Public

Reflect on "The Troubles"

Compiled by
Joseph Sheehy and Joshua Schultz

With an Introduction by
Martin Lynch

Published by The New Belfast
Community Arts' Initiative

First published in N. Ireland in 2001 by
The New Belfast Community Arts' Initiative
15 Church Street, Belfast BT1 1PG

ISBN 0-9540662-0-0

Printed and bound by W & G Baird Ltd
Antrim, N. Ireland

Contents

Foreword   ix

I. THE POETS

Chris Agee	Port of Belfast	2
John Bradbury	Northern Ireland in the Sixties	3
Ruth Carr	Home	5
Gerald Dawe	Straws in the Wind	6
Seamus Deane	Phantoms, 1968–2001	7
Padraic Fiacc	Enemy encounters	8
Lily Fitzsimons	Recipe for a bright new future called Hope	9
Sadie Fox	Changes	10
Brendan Hamill	The long gig	11
Seamus Heaney	The Catechism	12
Michael Hilton	Aftermath	13
Paul Jeffcutt	City asleep	14
Fred Johnston	At Roselawn Cemetery (for my father)	15
Nathan ben Chaim Kripz	The Jew looks on	16
Michael Longley	Ceasefire	17
Joan McBreen	The Peace-keeper	18
Kathleen McCracken	Good Friday, Belfast, 1998	20
Peter McDonald	Least Harm	22
Brain Mac Gabhann	The Journey	23
Niall McGrath	Recollection	26
Medbh McGuckian	The Heart Ghost	27
Jacqui McMenamin	To and Fro	28
Martin Mooney	The War Effort	29
Paul Muldoon	The whitethorns	30
Bernard O'Donoghue	Islandmagee Castle	31
Padraig Ó Snodaigh	Do Rosalita	32
Tom Paulin	Mandelson installs Direct Rule	33
Grainne Tobin	That was then, this is now	34
Robert Welch	Inner City	35
Anne Zell	12th Morning, Falls Park	36

v

II. THE POLITICIANS

Yvonne Boyle	City on the lough	38
Joan Carson MLA	Equality	39
Ivan Davis MLA	Changing Belfast	40
Sam Foster MLA	A simple code	41
D. R. Hussey MLA	Is it not time?	42
Steve McBride	Belfast	43
Eliz Byrne McCullough	Northern Giant	44
Alex Maskey MLA	Time will Tell	45
Mary Nelis MLA	The older I get	46
Jim Wilson MLA	Face the truth	47

III. THE PUBLIC

Joseph Sheehy	Reflections on a life	49
The Bard of Belfast	Shifting sand	50
Eileen Clarke	New Belfast	51
Mark Cooper	From the outside	52
Maureen Harkins	See	53
David Cullen	The Ceasefire	54
David Cullen	Why?	55
David Cullen	Tell me why?	56
John S. Mercer	Phoenix	57
John S. Mercer	The search for peace	58
David Ferris	Secrets of Ben Madigan	59
Issy Osborne	Just peace	60
Hilary Fairleigh	The way we were	61
Sally Anne Swaffield	Starlight starbright	62
Lynne Graham	Falling apart	63
B. McAteer	Fidelity	64
Anne Smith	Joey	65
Anne Smith	Another soldier	66
John L. Peshkin	An aside	67
Joseph McCullough	Dreams	68
Lily McWilliams	Day out in Belfast	69
Lily McWilliams	Dockland child	70
Sonia Craven Haddad	Out of the window	71

Margaret Wilson	An East Belfast childhood	72
Shirley-Anne McMillan	The big man	73
Shirley-Anne McMillan	Your house	74
Bridget Logue	Time	75
Anonymous	Target	76
Neely McGrath	A leap of faith	77
Maureen Bunting	Thoughts on the past and future	78
Hazel Wilson	Belfast	79
Hazel Wilson	Two friends	80
Matthew Cosby	Take the 'Ire' from Ireland	81
Allison Hamilton	What's it all about?	82
Martin Magee	The syllables of change	83
Martin Magee	Catch a falling star	84
Henry Power	Remembrance	85
Henry Power	Aurora	86
Suzanne Hyman	My death	87
Harry Barry	Another solution	89
Rhonda Watson	New agreement	90
F. Jackson	The times they are a' changing	91
Carolyn Thompson	Lagan Weir	92
Paddy Murphy	Belfast	93
Paddy Murphy	Belfast	94
James Snoddy	Maternity ward	95
James Snoddy	Cancer City	96
Michael Little	Light on the Lagan	97
Brendan F. Magee	End Game?	98
John McKittrick	Colours	99
John Ritchie	Heading back	100
Harriet Brown	A prayer for peace	101
W. H. Lunn	Life	102
Joanna Braniff	Ireland: A Surrealist Study	103
Betty McIlroy	Changing face	104
Ita McMichael	Early transport	105
Sylvia Butcher	Learn to forgive	106
George Sproule	Kerbstone	107
Valerie Morrison	There's another side	108
Margaret Millar	Belfast mountains	109
Margaret Millar	Two little boys	110
Maureen R. Cunningham	The Voter's plea	111

Gerry Gallagher	Flyover	112
Chris McCrory	The best we could	113
Chris McCrory	Here and Now	114
Olivia Butler	We wish	115
Olivia Butler	And now	116
E. Vance	O how I love Belfast	117
Joe Ruane	Releasing	118
Katherine Martin	Walking Botanic	119
Hugh G. Rice	Advance	120
John Peshkin	A place apart?	121
Geraldine Reid	The walk	122
Alan Crawford	What days do you love the best?	123
Alan Crawford	It is Belfast	124
Julia Paul	The house	125
Fred McIlmoyle	Redundant	126
Fred McIlmoyle	Hope	127
Michael McConkey	No anahorish	128
Michael McConkey	Last night I met with Christ	129
Una Woods	Voices in jagged white	130
Una Woods	Coming words	131
Una Woods	The future is late tonight	132
Margaret Madden	The time of our lives	133
Ian C. Webb	Heat	134
Wilma Kenny	Belfast	135
Robert Corrigan	Hope	136
Michael Mulholland	Wise words	137
Michael Mulholland	Reconstruction	138
Ann Cassidy	Belfast	139
Carolyn Hall	In this place	140
F. Bunting	Life's journey	141
F. Bunting	The ageing process	142
Andrew D. Glover	Ocean bridge	143
Yvonne Henry	Childsplay	144
Jay Boreen	Face up	145
Jane Grace	People of war	146
Jane Grace	A little reminder	147
Jane Grace	Just like me	148
Jane Grace	Journey	149
Joyce Finlay	Prozac tanto quid	150

Foreword

Artistes Need Communities,
Communities Need Artistes
The New Power of the Arts

I remember years ago, Michael Longley – now unquestionably our most illus-
trious resident poet in Northern Ireland – saying that he felt the politicians here
were failing the people. He went further and said he thought it would be up to
the artistes in our community to forge a new dialogue to help resolve the trou-
bles in Northern Ireland. At the time, I thought he was a crackpot, off his head,
probably taking tablets – that's what I thought at the time.

Today, I'm not so sure.

When we reflect on some of the theatre work that has been produced over
the last twenty or so years, we can begin to see how a dialogue was, and has
been, in fact taking place. If you look at the plays of Graham Reid, Christina
Reid, myself, Charabanc Theatre Company, etc. in the 80's, it has to be recog-
nised that large numbers of people from all sections of our community went to
see these plays, not just in conventional theatres but in community centres,
social clubs, leisure centres, etc. – in the very heart of communities. These plays
had the power to make people laugh, to move them and to create debate long
after the final curtain. In the 90's, we could look on the work of Dubblejoint
Theatre Company, Marie Jones and Just Us and the packed houses they played
to in the heart of West Belfast. The political dialogue – or propaganda – what-
ever takes your fancy – was clearly palpable and, above all, relevant.

In my opinion, The Wedding Community Play which took place throughout
1998/1999, took this kind of political dialogue to a new level. The very people
from the most troubled areas of Belfast – and all the personal and family con-
nections, hurts, prejudices, rivalries, traditions, etc. that that entailed – came
together and entered into a dialogue about the nature of their society. It was
blunt, humourous, painful, joyous, enlightening, life-changing, etc. – and that
was before a word was spoken on stage! We know The Wedding Community
Play didn't change the world, but perhaps it changed something for the fifty

participants who felt that this medium – the medium of the arts – was a real and tangible way to debate and articulate their lives. This kind of dialogue and debate would simply not have happened in these communities twenty, thirty, or forty years ago. Without community theatre, these people have to rely on our politicians engaging – in the main – in a kind of arm's length, emotionally-arrested war mode, flinging and flying of words, ideas and insults.

Perhaps the other art forms have not been so successful in creating a dialogue within the Northern Ireland community.

For instance, in spite of the politically provocative work of some of our best known visual artistes, such as Joe McWilliams, Dermot Seymour, Jack Packenham, the Delargeys, etc., in my opinion, their work has not reached significant levels of public debate and dialogue, largely because of the preponderance of showing the work in conventional spaces. Spaces that are forever doomed to be inhabited only by the adventurous, the moderately temperate, anger-sealed few. It could be argued that the work of politically motivated street muralists, such as Danny Devanny, has had more of an impact on the city of Belfast than all the aforementioned artistes put together.

Only the work of Rita Duffy stands out as a politically engaging artiste who is not only concerned with the content of her work but – and this is crucial – is concerned enough to ensure her work is seen by a wide section of the population in unconventional spaces and places.

Disappointingly, it might be concluded by most that the work of our best known poets has not had the kind of impact on society that it might have up to this point. I say this, knowing poetry will never rival football in the popularity stakes. Heaney is an obvious exception, in that he is popularly read and exposed to large numbers of young people at school level. His politically orientated poems have been few and far between and he would never gain a political mantle. The best known of the others – e.g., Muldoon, Mahon, Montague, McGuckian, Paulin, Carson, etc. – have largely written, it might be argued, into some kind of large underground pipe that is not visible to the vast majority of the people of Northern Ireland. Here, I think, Michael Longley has the potential and the power to transcend all of this. He is reaching a stage where his work is becoming 'popular'; and, above all, he shows a keen interest in being relevant. The next five years will be interesting.

Against my better judgement, I am coming round to Michael Longley's point of view regarding the possible impact of artistes on real life in Northern Ireland.

However, I probably come at this from a different angle to Longley. As a consequence of my work, both in the mainstream arts and community arts, I now firmly believe that in order for art to mean anything to large numbers of people, there must be an engagement by the artiste with the community. Obviously, since I believe art, in all its forms, enhances and civilises us, both as individuals and as communities, I am equally certain that communities need artistes.

When the Belfast European Partnership Board announced its funding criteria for its second tranche of Peace 1 funds three years ago, it stipulated a preference for applications that were (i) citywide and (ii) proposed by a consortium of groups. This created debate within the Community Arts forum. We finally decided that we would form a consortium and apply. We also decided that our project would be called **The 'New Belfast' Community Arts' Initiative**. The Initiative would involve five separate but linked projects:

Poetry in Motion – an attempt to get the people of Belfast to send poems to each other instead of bullets.

Strangers Next Door – the idea that young people living in the immediate vicinity of our peace walls would articulate their lives via the taking of photographs.

The Belfast Wheel – the notion that groups within communities would create a mosaic or piece of public art that could be joined to other pieces of art to make a citywide installation in the centre of Belfast.

The Hall of Fame – the creation of dozens of larger-than-life puppets based on Belfast folk heroes for use in carnival parades and festivals.

Football Mad – a large scale Community Play looking at the rivalries between the supporters of Cliftonville and Linfield football clubs.

We called it The 'New Belfast' Community Arts' Initiative because we had the clear intent of creating a dialogue among the people of Belfast via the arts, that might articulate the new, post-thirty-years-of-troubles Belfast. If there is to be a 'new Belfast' (and God knows we deserve it), we felt the arts could play a significant role. We believed in the new power of the arts to get in among the most affected areas and create a new dialogue and possibly change. Time will tell if we made any kind of impact.

This book, which I am honoured to write the foreword to, is a direct, tangible manifestation of the Poetry in Motion Project. Within these pages you will see – literally – a community in dialogue with itself. Poems instead of bullets. Metaphors instead of insults. Hopes instead of hatred. This book – with its unique collection of established poets, politicians and ordinary people, addressing the conflict of the last thirty years *and* looking to the future – represents a one-off. It has never been done before and I doubt it will ever come round again. I believe we are indebted to Lizzie Devlin and all at the New Belfast Community Arts' Initiative for making it possible, to Deirdre McBride and the board of the Belfast European Partnership Board for taking a huge gamble to support an 'arts' project; and, last but not least, to the indefatigable Joe Sheehy and Josh Schultz for guiding the Poetry in Motion project with such wild enthusiasm and belief. The new power of the arts indeed.

Martin Lynch, Writer & Co-ordinator of The Community Arts Forum

I.
THE POETS

PORT OF BELFAST

Hung on a wall of Calvinist stars,
the moon is a mottled goatskin bodhran,
a vellum of weathered light
above the fog and frost of Lagan dips.

Chris Agee,
Belfast

NORTHERN IRELAND IN THE SIXTIES
A Child's Perception

There was always a hint
Of us and them ...
Some intangible difference
Separate schools
Different way of life.

They lived down the road.
Met up from time to time.
Didn't know what to say ...
BE nice ... be nice.
Going to see the Parades today?
You enquired in a fairly
Half-hearted way.

But then it was different
No threatening undercurrent
Not so menacing ... more fun.

I lived in the country,
Moving to the town
As the Troubles began.

Living in suburbia
Protected from the realities
Of fermenting unrest.

Images on a TV screen,
Wrapped in a middle class cocoon.
Images of violence loom.

Dwarfed in my perception
By a man on the moon.
More concerned with Brian Jones
And the rest of the Rolling Stones.
Beatles and Georgie Best
Was fast becoming a mess.

I was too concerned
With the Wednesday play,
Football in the park,
Autumn leaves tumbling
Rushing homework after dark.

Black and white TV
European Cup pennants,
Somehow the violence just
Didn't make sense.

Hey, boy! Are you a Fenian?

No need for elaborate pretence.
Just point at a school badge
Mutter in the negative.

Shuffle home for early tea.
Try hard not to show offence.

John Bradbury,
Belfast

HOME

If I was not from here
I might believe that what they say is
all there is to you
I might believe I held the answer
in my pocket
I might believe

But being from your clay
I know I do not know the half
of it.
I know I only hold crumbs in my hand
or stones
to cast upon your river's mouth
and stay.

Ruth Carr,
Belfast

STRAWS IN THE WIND

I sleep in my daughter's bed tonight
while she snortles feverishly by her mother.
Her things are all around me.
I am like a giant in a doll's house
and in the mirror of her dressing-table
see myself, ludicrous with glasses on,
a cursèd fly buzzing overhead.

If I had the choice what could I hope for?
That she see this night through with ease
and that her dreams suffice
so when morning comes
the sickness will have passed.
But now, with time on my hands,
I wish for her much more –

the passion and caress of love;
the want to go on, not just saving face.
Far better she just sleeps.
In the meantime, like standing guard,
I think I hear night-things bombard
our fragile peace: straws in the wind,
a fugitive dog sniffing the backsteps.

Gerald Dawe,
Dublin

PHANTOMS, 1968–2001

The churches are burning,
Flamingoes standing in the air;
A fly melts in the liqueur
Of its dying along the window,
And a map comes smoking in the post
In a heat-wraithed parcel.
Rain has wept, wind sworn,
There's not a soul about.
Phantoms are beating
     On the door,
     Beating to get out.

While a toy and beautiful ship
Straightens within a bottle
A phone is lifted like a knife
And left to sing a decapitated
Tone. Ramparts of high air
Are climbing into flames longing
For oxygen. There's not a soul
About. Phantoms are beating
     On the door,
     Beating to get out.

Seamus Deane,
Dublin

7

ENEMY ENCOUNTERS

i

At the Gas and Electric
                    Offices
Black boats with white sails
Float down the stairs
Frighten the five year old
Wee protestant girls.

'Nuns, nuns,' one of them yells
'When are yez gon' to git
                           married?'

ii

Dumping (left over from the autumn)
Dead leaves, near a culvert
I come on
          a British Army Soldier
With a rifle and a radio
Perched hiding. He has red hair.

He is young enough to be my weenie
–bopper daughter's boy friend.
He is like a lonely little winter robin.

We are that close to each other, I
Can nearly hear his heart beating.

I say something bland to make him grin,
But his glass eyes look past my side
–whiskers down
                the Shore Road street.

I am an Irish man
                  and he is afraid
That I have come to kill him.

Padraic Fiacc,
Belfast

RECIPE FOR A BRIGHT NEW FUTURE
CALLED HOPE

First we need a large helping of
Good will and trust to start
Throw in mutual respect
An open mind and heart
Mix with love and determination
Success is a wonderful sensation
Hope will rise like a cloud
Sometimes dark and threatening
Then a gesture of good faith
Comes to brighten our day
Remember a little hope and
Trust can go a long, long way.

Lily Fitzsimons,
Belfast

CHANGES.

Such a change has come about
No more R.U.C. shouts of out, out, out.
No bin lids pounding a warning sound
Not everyone will stand his or her ground.

The change they say, was brought through peace
Yet the troubles to me will never cease.
This peace deal seems to me not right
When I am woken in the night.

Screeching brakes, horns blasting a tune
Every night a new full moon.
It's not the loyalists running amok, going mad
Nor British soldiers' wrecking and ruining that leaves us sad.

It's our own children causing the storm
Hooded monsters intent on harm.
Youngsters left on the streets to run
I fear our troubles have just begun.

Sadie Fox,
Belfast

THE LONG GIG

The long gig started slowly when I was twenty-one
Poetry helped to keep me sane
If not immune.

The long gig
Left so many watermarks
Invisible cities within cities

'Graveyards in the gut'
Sodden with grief,

The last posts---
Yet people cannot live with ghosts forever

No matter how the tide turns
Causes come and go in time.

Keep your eye fixed
On the metallic blue light

Of that unnameable star
Which doesn't want or need a label.

Auden said it all in the white hot thirties,
"Love or perish," distrust all dogmatic prigs,

Hold all Easts and Wests free from fear
Close only the door.

When snowflakes fall
They become one, a genderless purity.

Renew the face of the earth
When the ballroom is empty

Listen to the sound of your own heartbeat
It's been a long gig.

Brendan Hamill,
Belfast

THE CATECHISM

Q. and A. come back. They formed my mind.
"Who is my neighbour?" "My neighbour is all mankind."

Seamus Heaney,
Dublin

AFTERMATH

A black cloth cross
Was fixed to the door
And people came, in and out,
In and out for three days.

Men came with a flag
To drape the coffin with.
'He died for his country,' they said,
over and over, over and over
for three days.

Many faces touched his mother
In remorseful gestures.
Voices, in repetitive whispers, echoed
'I'm sorry for your loss', again and again,
again and again for three days.

And yet, with all the fuss,
She heard no other voice
Or saw no other face but his,
Looking up from sleep. 'Asleep, not dead;
Asleep, not dead,' she said, for three days.

Michael Hilton,
Belfast

CITY ASLEEP

The dream is an end,
the end is another dream.,
begin to dream.

Paul Jeffcutt,
Belfast

AT ROSELAWN CEMETERY
(:for my father:)

Stooping in snow to uncover
My father's headstone unmarked
With his life and death,
I felt the blow of being someone else.

Not a son now, not in a sense
That reels out of photographs, or
Carries memory like a battery-lamp
In the pockets of his going about.

More a tourist in a proposition
Of a country, a possibility,
Where dead names are markers
On every map, in every guidebook.

And so my compass-pointer sheers
Off the anticipated towards the true,
Snagged on the crosspoint of years –
Roselawn Cemetery, the sky arctic blue.

Fred Johnston,
Galway

THE JEW LOOKS ON

The Jew looks on

this is not his war
   his peace
the land that tore him
   screeching
      from his mother's womb
which forced him to live
   to breathe
     to think
an eternal stranger
a reject without a nation

he's never been to Israel
   his home is here
     this Irish Jew

Nathan ben Chaim Kripz,
Belfast

CEASEFIRE

I

Put in mind of his own father and moved to tears
Achilles took him by the hand and pushed the old king
Gently away, but Priam curled up at his feet and
Wept with him until their sadness filled the building.

II

Taking Hector's corpse into his own hands Achilles
Made sure it was washed and, for the old king's sake,
Laid out in uniform, ready for Priam to carry
Wrapped like a present home to Troy at daybreak.

III

When they had eaten together, it pleased them both
To stare at each other's beauty as lovers might,
Achilles built like a god, Priam good-looking still
And full of conversation, who earlier had sighed:

IV

'I get down on my knees and do what must be done
And kiss Achilles' hand, the killer of my son.'

Michael Longley,
Belfast

THE PEACE-KEEPER

Dedicated to the memory of Aonghus Murphy, killed on
active service with the Unifil troops in Lebanon, August 1986

The soldier's
dark-haired girl
had never seen

the scorching
Lebanon
sun

beat
its furious heat
on the yellow hills.

She did not hear
the screech
or flap

of frightened birds
or see them
fly

senseless
in the smoke-filled
sky.

She did not hear
the soldiers
there

curse and swear
before
they filled

the humid foreign
air
with cries.

And when
her peace-keeper's body
came home

no coolin airs
or purple-heathered
August haze

over brown
midland bogs
softened
the treachery.

No Army dirge,
or flags at half-mast
in silent
towns,

no sympathy,
or priest's gentle words
could change

her lament to lullaby,
or keen
him

ever from the damp
sea-salted
Galway soil.

Joan McBreen,
Galway

GOOD FRIDAY, BELFAST, 1998

i.

Later in the day
Our daughter says
The snow is an angel's wing
Folded over Knockagh,
Or the tongue of an ox
Licking salt.

At 6 a.m. I found you
Walking in sleep, trying
To make sense of a dream
About a soldier
Knee-deep in Brueghel's
Massacre of the Innocents.

My own dream
Was smaller:
Three gentle men
And a lady
Sitting to draughts
In a moated castle.

We are all
Dreaming the same dream.

ii.

I am squinting down the shaft
Of a splintered telescope, trying to catch
A glimpse of the goings-on
Over at Stormont.

Your eyes are wide open,
Gaze back at the camera, saying:
Everything is in motion,
Still.

We are waiting for a sign, for the idiom
To cut a new skin, the language
To alter so dramatically
It acquires a new vocabulary.

Not an execution, but miracles.
Not fixity, but faith.
Nothing but the bottom line

Will satisfy the look of honesty
On the face of that young man
And the woman old enough to be his mother

The pair of them
Standing like the rest of us
Up to our oxters in snow, in salt.

Aren't we all
Dreaming the same dream?

Kathleen McCracken,
Greenisland

LEAST HARM

Enough just to be there,
taken right down, apart
to the frame just, the skeleton,
barely there,
enough to say it enough of that
whatever else again,
but there just, whatever
good it is or it does.

Peter McDonald,
Christ Church,
Oxford.

THE JOURNEY

There, in the handling of a person
Is the depth of where we are
So far back in time
Through the duration of a wisdom
To that point of vision and insightfulness

For from the blood we plead
There is a cry to venture
Not more in that path of hate
But down a road of human care
Where we may say -
This is how we go

There in the words we choose
Is the vein that takes us forward
Not speech that leaves us stabbed by ignorance
But by human utterance,
That shows good use of thought

So simple is it to cross swords
Yet when we do
We are drawn away
To other times, bereft of human love

That other pasture we must seek
That plain, where finally we lay
Our slicing steel

And open up our hearts
To bring our following breed along
To set up roots for them and more

For from the blood we plead
Take us beyond the cries,
To live anew

No more of vicious times
Wherein no love of ours can settle
Wherein no child we know can play

Take us beyond the yoke of years of pain
And put us down by wisdom's hand,
More civilised of thought

For that is what our thought is for
To take us further than our time
To be a guide to a proper goal
Where we can feel we've moved ahead

And though it's said –
It's not like ancient times in Greece
When language and philosophy
Found their own broad road

But, yet – it is –
For like the Greeks
We too are now employed
In movement of the same

For we as well
Have known the weaponry of war
When blood had flown and
Milked all innocence of life's great licence
When anger was no friend of thought
To cool it down or chase with quick remorse
When friendships were selective
And human hearts, that did not mature,
Stood divided of a love
That was for all by right
When kindness was not free to find its way
But was grounded by the hatred
That crossed the land
Its cloak upon so many backs
That it cursed some sad life in every street
When memory was choked by grievance of a few

That no sun shone in to mellow vicious imagery
Like the harvest time that blesses us
And yet to many, is not a gift of nature

That gives us sustenance
For some will only take and take
And never see the great fortune of existence
As it touches us

For some will only live and die
So unaware of other levels
That surround them
And yet they will be passed,
As weed beneath the wheel,
By man, in that slow crawl of time
That brings us forward,
From mausoleum to the finest dust
Burial in the earth beside a healthy rose

From ignorance and tragedy
To times of richer hearts and thoughts
Where emotion plays the smaller part
Within the act
And humanity proceeds,
Not shrouded, like before,
In begrudgery of hate

For from the blood we plead
From the searing flying metal we cry
From the agony
And last tears on our victim's face
From the broken hearts
Of the painfully bereaved

We stand
We stand, oh God
Our hands outstretched

We stand
Ready to go forward
As bearers of the flag of
The reconciled

Brian Mac Gabhann,
Belfast

RECOLLECTION

The fascination of dinky cars
Is disrupted by a Newsflash:
Squatting on the rug, he watches
As a priest on the TV screen
Crouches, waves a bloody hankie.
He frowns: Derry's not far.
Turning back, his toys about to crash,
The child guides them
Out of harm's way.

Niall McGrath
Ballyclare

THE HEART GHOST

A dream stood over me
Attracted by the lamplight
Out of sight – a shredded
Face that came back from
The dead of its own accord

To carry out the living. Only
Its head was visible, the
Shelves of brow and chin
As if preserved in redress, like
A Prussian town now in Poland.

Medbh McGuckian,
Belfast

TO AND FRO

Two seats in front of me
On the bus to Belfast
A Rosetti painting reflected in the glass

As we came near Dungannon, she pulled
Her bronze gold hair, into a velvet scrunchy,
With squat, milk white fingers.
She stared out at the lake and smiled at
The ducks and swans as I did.

I wondered if she knew how
Beautiful she was,
How beguiling.
In dark blue denim.

The journey back was not so pleasant.
The bus driver had a dangerous looking, dangly earring
And a pair of wrap around sunglasses.
With his shaved head he looked like a terrorist.

The only seat was at the back and it creaked all the way to
Ballygawley, when I grabbed a seat as far away as possible.
I tried to read the poetry review, but ended up thinking of
How broadly you smiled when you saw me.
Your cheerful "Hallo" and that green jumper
I'd burn if I got my hands on it.

Never did get inside your comfort zone
Invade that personal space.
Get that horrible jumper off you and
Conveniently lose it.

Jacqui McMenamin,
Omagh

THE WAR EFFORT

The aldermen had melted the railings for cannon, but now
They haggled over a waste of ratepayers' money
Suggesting instead a new fire-engine or a public park;
Until a few of the men on the dole and a couple of boys –
There are always corner-boys in an escapade like this –
Scraped together a plinth of snow, and a snow-soldier
Sporting a veteran's tin hat, coal-eyes, and a wooden rifle.

Which shamed the aldermen into raising the funds
For this, our dour memorial, though hundreds like it
Stand in hospital foyers, train-station platforms and schools;
Which you read like history, scanning the list of names
For a name like your own, forgetting that sculptors
And foundries have to be paid, that limestone and brass,
Because they last longer than snow, cost hard-earned money.

Martin Mooney,
Belfast

WHITETHORNS

The paling-posts we would tap into the ground with the flat of a spade
more than thirty years ago,
hammering them home then with a sledge
and stringing them with wire to keep our oats from Miller's barley,

are maxed out, multilayered whitethorns, affording us a broader, deeper shade
than we ever decently hoped to know,
so farfetched does it seem, so farflung from the hedge
under which we now sit down to parley.

Paul Muldoon,
Princeton, USA

ISLANDMAGEE CASTLE

For James Simmons

It is a castle, according to the map,
and you can find your way to it by climbing through
from the Crawfords' cattle-sheds. Right enough,
it has a Norman-looking arch over the gap
which must be where the window was, though now
it's just six feet of stone, barely hanging
together. The calves are nudging at
the hay-wisps round its base, oblivious to

What lies behind them: oyster-catchers
crying down at the shingle beach; sheer blue
between them and the green of Portmuck island,
and Ailsa Craig beyond. Once I stumbled
through there, trying to keep my feet, and found myself
face-to-face with a furtive-looking character,
his double-breasted coat hugged close around him.
'A gun,' I thought. He opened his coat

Revealing a colander of mushrooms.
'Take as many as you want for your northern fry,'
he said. 'Sure the fields are full of them this weather.'

Bernard O'Donoghue,
Wadham College,
Oxford

DO ROSALITA

'Ti amo Agnese'
Graffito in Roma
E dico ancora.

Padraig Ó Snodaigh,
Dublin

MANDELSON INSTALLS DIRECT RULE

Either a countdown or a lull
either a death throe or that desul–
tory that dull shallow neapness
except it's a tad unreal
this line in the sand this deadline
where everything after must fail
– what I regret is the loss
of the educational genius
of Martin McGuinness
– he'd have dropped the 11+
the whole sectarian
and therefore necessitarian
system of training
the minds of the young
and imagine all those smug feepaying
schools taxed out of existence
swept off the face of the province!
– the Minister's loss is still unsung
– direct rule
means the same ould skules.

Tom Paulin,
Oxford

THAT WAS THEN, THIS IS NOW

Daffodils bought from a bucket
on the sleety pavement,
their poke of greengrocer's paper
an inhalation mask
dizzying me back
to that pale bay-windowed room,
your jug of early daffodils
sounding a declaration –
wild gold bells, dusted with pollen,
loud, saturated yellow,
scenting the uncertain light.

Grainne Tobin,
Newcastle, Co. Down

INNER CITY

The bar is called The Grapes.
'Of Wrath' is daubed in black
on the wall of the porch. The wall
is painted a blue hard-gloss.

Inside, quivering in the teak
of a wooden counter you'd never see
your face in, is a stainless steel
cook's knife, handle and blade all
cast in one solid piece. Turning
in the air, having been thrown
from the doorway to the jakes
over the baize of the pool table,
a revolver. Caught, and deftly
affianced to the hand, the finger
finds the soft curve of the trigger,
before thumping it down on the bar.

The barkeep, with the gold solidus
round his neck, tweaks once more
the smooth handle of the knife to hear
it hum, as, in the porch, in the gathering rain,
the blond girl from the south takes shelter.

Robert Welch,
University of Ulster

12th MORNING, FALLS PARK

Tearaways on mountain bikes
yodel down the river path.
Twins ascend the hill

resplendent
in a double buggy
with a fringe on top.

The river is low
and full of junk, but
it gurgles, satisfactorily

past a primitive forest
of horsetail ferns, rhododendrons
stealing a march

feathery trees
the ivy's claimed
for climbing frames.

Helicopters
have all gone south
for the day. I sit

on the stump of a tree
that outlived its civic function
thinking

poetry will not
save us. Writing it
anyway.

Ann Zell,
Belfast

36

II
THE POLITICIANS

CITY ON THE LOUGH

City on the lough
Cultural intersection of many times and tides

Our mosaic solution of peace
Shows the glistening pieces of past goals and pain
Set in a matrix of hope

Looking at the sky
Where the sea meets the hills
We can say
We have lived the depths
We are making real the vision of the heights.

Yvonne Boyle,
Alliance Party Spokesperson
on Arts, Culture and Heritage

EQUALITY

American images
Flashed on screens.
Righteous discontent brings
Turbulent crowds
Demanding equality.

Aped here but twisted
For political gain.
Murders, maiming
Bombing, deaths
To gain equality?

Stop! Enough!
Cried the people.
This suffering is unjustified.
Respect for our differences
Is true equality.

Joan Carson, UUP
Fermanagh and S. Tyrone

CHANGING BELFAST

You wouldn't know old Belfast now
From Belfast long ago;
There's such a change from Royal Avenue
Right down to Sandy Row;
There's jewellers and restaurants
And seats to sit you down;
That's if you could get near them, for
The young lads of the town!

There's quite a change the bombers made
But not the change they meant;
For things that they did mean for harm
Turned out for betterment;
Of places that had stood for years
You couldn't find a trace
They're blown away and built anew
You wouldn't know the place;

There's litter bins and litter louts
And ne'er the twain shall meet;
If only they would take a thought
And tidy up the street;
For this place is their heritage
A place of old renown;
For change may come and change may go
It's still old Belfast town.

Ivan Davis, Ulster Unionist,
Lagan Valley

A SIMPLE CODE

No grumbling, no sulking, no feuding, no fighting,
But looking and looking for things to delight in,
No hating the state of the world every minute,
But seeking and finding the beauty that's in it,
No worrying and letting your troubles confound you,
But laughing and liking the people around you.

Presented by Sam Foster,
Minister of the Environment,
Stormont

IS IT NOT TIME?

Is it not time that you city folk learned
Of those of us further afield?
Get into the car, the train or a bus,
You'll be surprised what joys it can yield,
And when we make the trip on up to your town,
Perhaps upon us you'll no longer frown!

D.R. Hussey, UUP
West Tyrone.

BELFAST

Above the streets, the hills.
Above the people, the sky.
Belfast.

Councillor Steve McBride,
Alliance

NORTHERN GIANT

There you are.
There you are, a giant resting
Along the northern edge of Belfast.
A wind cheater, a mist maker, a forest shaker;
Long and strong against a sky of swimming-pool blue.

Rose brick houses shelter as near as they dare.
Those rose houses are our houses.
This giant is our giant.
So there you are.
There you are and here I am
Struck still on Victoria Street,
Just looking at you.

Elizabeth Byrne McCullough,
Secretary, Women's Coalition

TIME WILL TELL

Don't ask or even ponder,
30 years what a wonder!
30 plus it seems to me since the world
began to see,
Malcolm X and Cohn-Bendit –
Here at home – we'll have to end it.

Alex Maskey, Sinn Fein
West Belfast

THE OLDER I GET

The older I get the more I marvel
at whats always been around
The formation of clouds, the multi-coloured sky
The wind a symphony of sound
The older I get the more I learn
of a world where riches abound
The feel of the grass, the sound of the sea
Life, light, energy an inheritance new found
The older I get...

Mary Nelis, Sinn Fein
Derry

FACE THE TRUTH

Turn around and face the truth
Hidden from you in your youth
By leaders who tried your mind to sway
That their truth was the only way.

Turn around and face the truth
Hidden from you in your youth
Question those who say to you
That none but them had a point of view.

Turn around and face the truth
Hidden from you in your youth
By people who played upon your fear
To benefit them in their career.

Turn around and face the truth
Hidden from you in your youth
And see a future for all to enjoy
Every woman, man, girl and boy.

Jim Wilson, UUP
South Antrim

III
THE PUBLIC

REFLECTIONS ON A LIFE

Kneecapped at five
By too much prayer
To a God who never was
Prisoner of their tabernacle
Lectured, beaten
Allowed to be
Provisionally
By men in masks
And clerical frocks
She beckons to me
This Survivor God
Fifty years on...

Joseph Sheehy,
Newtownabbey

SHIFTING SAND

The people of Belfast have been through the mill.
From the top of Blackmountain
To the foot of Shankill.

They have mourned and cried and drowned in their tears
Through the loss of their loved ones mowed down through the years.
The blood of our children screams out from the land
Whilst political decisions keep shifting like sand.

Like actors in a video we bury our dead.
The same gaunt faces, the same words said.
We follow the coffins with unquestioned fate
Following the horror we helped to create.

Those left behind are sick with despair
Far removed from the spotlight and the media glare.
Do we want to know them or do we even care
As their grief gets harder and heavier to bear?

We have to stop before it's too late.
This lust for blood has to abate.
We cannot afford to lose our young.
They are the song of love yearning to be sung.

If there is a God I hope he will hear
The voices of those who live in fear.
Then He will lift his Healing hand
And breathe strength into our shifting sand.

The Bard of Belfast

NEW BELFAST

Man makes house with bricks and stone
<u>Homes</u> are made with love alone
Homes are built with loving care
With hands that help and hearts that share
Where quarrels are sorted and life goes on
With grudges forgotten in laughter and song
Where all are treated fair and square
With respect for all who are living there
This is <u>your</u> home so build it well
So generations to come can tell
That all lived here content and free
A family – together in harmony.

Eileen Clarke,
Kircubbin

FROM THE OUTSIDE

Work at last!
Belfast.
Images haunt needs.
Cruel, senseless deeds.

That was then and now is now.
Five years I've seen, four years my wife.
We've listened, learned, experienced,
Peace.

And now our Belfast girl is born.
Into a community,
warm but worn.
I pray she'll want her home.

Mark Cooper,
Belfast.

52

SEE

No distance from her contentment
Far removed by Blindness
A lapse of time replenished
Her eyes no longer blighted
She has witnessed deceit
Gone from the chains that bound her
Found again in sweet seclusion

Maureen Harkins,
Ballybeen

THE CEASEFIRE

Look at my friend, whom,
I don't even know.
Young man full of promise,
With me he will go.
Companion today – but will it last?
Live for the future,
What's gone is the past.

No more guns; no more bombs,
No more running away.
For now we have peace.
And God let it stay.
For should it break down,
We must stay true and through.
I knew not you my friend,
But now it is true.

So peace now forever,
For ever all more.
For I have forgiven.
Like so does the shore.
Choosing no side of people,
Washes all through and through.
The sea knows no evil,
One people all more.

Mem-or-ies of today,
Seem so far away.
Those of years ago,
So near today.

David Cullen,
Belfast

WHY?

My friend he did die, but does he know?
He fought for us all, but who remembers?
He wore his cross across his back,
He could not see his children.
His wife cries alone, sure it killed his mother.
And, God, look at us, he died for Ireland.

The streets were in red,
An unsaid decade of the Rosary.
Bus as always one, united we stand, united we fell.
But now altogether, let's all stand as one.

My fists now are open, the tables are turned.
The terror is finished, no more bombs, no more guns.
Turn off the telly and sit by the fire.
The fighting's all over, come together as one.

But is there a spy there?
Are we really safe?
We still hate the peelers, they still have their guns.

David Cullen,
Belfast

TELL ME WHY

Black smoke, burnt cars,
    Smell the same.
Youth Clubs closed; children lost.
    What's their crime?

The Guinness gone, a policeman's cry,
    A mother's son is left to die.
A British soldier says hello.
    What's his name? A day goes by.

Men go to work, and so do I.
    What's the crime, a bird flies by.
God save my soul, before I die.
    I rot in jail, I did no crime.

A mother's day – Goes by, Goes by,
    She grows old, now it's '99.
Now I am free, like a bird I fly,
    Yet nothing to do, Now what's my crime.

Like a tree grows up,
    So do I.
A tree falls down.
    But I never die.
By God I stand,
    And ask him why.
No answer got,
    Just passed me by.

David Cullen,
Belfast

PHOENIX

Forget the strife, suspicion, fear
With which we view each other,
By learning to forgive we learn
To call each other brother.
Look round you – see the changes here
Wake up to all that's new;
Advantages abound, supplied
For all – not just the few.
Our little country rises up
A Phoenix from the fire,
Grasp this one chance with both your hands –
Achieve your heart's desire.

John S. Mercer,
Newtownabbey

THE SEARCH FOR PEACE

What is peace?
Peace of mind?
Peace to live our lives
unhindered by the whims
the interference
of our fellow men?

The heather covered mountains
or far off verdant valleys
where we might trek in search of peace,
are temporary.
For even here
the peace eventually palls
and we begin to miss
participation
in the outside world.

A life of quiet contemplation,
of our being,
an inward journey
to discover a sweet solace,
can conjure up demons,
monsters which lie dormant in our psyche
emerge to trouble our peace.
We cannot detach ourselves
from ourselves.
For we create our own disorder
passions –
though sometimes sweet,
can lead to misery and pain.

Is peace a *process*
by which those who've been taught to hate
become transformed?
Can they rise up
from the ashes of their sin,
shake off the gaudy clothes of prejudice
and learn to love their neighbours as themselves.

Perhaps through caring for each other,
forgetting selfishness
we'll find true peace.

John S. Mercer,
Newtownabbey

58

SECRETS OF BEN MADIGAN

Who would have thought a volcano lay beneath
Those rolling hills and mountain heath
That tower over the city of terraced homes
Yet maybe clans and chiefs did roam
The valleys and lanes and lanes again
That twist around Ben Madigan.

Who would have guessed a fort kept watch
Of raths and huts with roofs of thatch?
The years have dimmed our recollection
About Celts and Picts and Scots connections
And what secrets does she hold yet still
That mound known and loved as old Cave Hill?

David Ferris,
Newtownabbey

JUST PEACE

For years our land has been covered in blood
Like many shamrocks that grow in the mud
The cries from mothers for husbands and sons
Lives ended needlessly with bomb and guns.

Tears of young and old alike
As Death comes like a thief in the night
Which destroys young and robs the old
By wicked men whose hearts have grown cold.

Our Emerald Isle wants peace to last
Not to keep looking at mistakes from the past
All terrorism and hatred must cease
We don't want the pot of gold, just peace.

Issy Osborne,
Belfast

THE WAY WE WERE.

In days long gone, in Belfast City,
The "Plaza" was the haunt of many,
Office girls rushed out to dance,
The lunch-time break away, and prance,
Like animals released from cages,
They whirled and burled to Rockin' Elvis,
Hayley's Comets featured too,
And Matt Monroe, he crooned 'The Blues',
Then all too soon it was all over,
And back to work – until tomorrow!!

Dirndl skirts were all the fashion,
Pony tails and nets a' flashin',
Spongy sneakers, velvet collars,
Long 'drain pipes' were oh! So! Dashin!
"What ever next?" my mother sighed,
seeing the brand new jeans, I'd dyed,
Dad said, "You're never wearing that!
It's far too short and you're too fat!"
Teddy boys and Teddy girls,
At war with Mods and Rockers,
Motor bikes and leather gear,
And brightly coloured scooters.

Duffle coats in shades of camel,
Davy Crockett skull caps,
The tail hung down the rider's back,
In stripes of furry pattern,
I could write on for hours and hours,
Of all the things I've done,
I've lots and lots more things to do,
I'm only sixty-one!

M/s Hilary Fairleigh,
Belfast

STARLIGHT STARBRIGHT

The first star that
I wish on tonight:
For this city to hold
Peace and finally unite.

To walk out the door
And feel at ease
For this "bloody War"
To finally cease.

Forget bloodshed
Old and new
Try to forgive, for peace
Of mind it will give you.

And bring together
What is good and bad
The children, our future
Will not grow up to be sad.

And no more victims
This city will hold
Let's all go forward
Advance, don't be sold.

No more heartache
No more woe
Feel freedom in our streets
And not have to lie low.

Help the next generation
To create their own future
And together they will
Make a better teacher.

Ms Sally Anne Swaffield,
Belfast

FALLING APART

Bombs going off, filled people with fear.
Don't go to town, trouble is near,
Another man shot in the head.
People were wary, too many are dead.
Days of the Troubles, times were bleak.
"What's your religion?" No one would speak
Fear gripping in every heart.
Every day, this country was falling apart.
We need a bright future for our children
To grow, in peace and harmony, that's all
They should know.
No more bitterness, hatred, or tears
We've had enough this last 30 years.

Lynn Graham,
Belfast.

FIDELITY

Black cloak flapping,
he sat collecting
impervious to storm,
on cold unyielding steps.
Though balaclava clad
no terrorist he,
no need of strident call
"For God and Ulster",
'Twas plain he loved them both,
that humble lad from Shankill,
Belfast's own "Black Santa".

Mrs. B. McAteer,
Portglenone

JOEY

We listened that morning to all the acclaim
Of stranger and friend praising your name.
We watched all of Ulster united in grief
In memory of you we had one day of peace.
What an honour to you, your family, your wife
If Catholic and Protestant were united in life.
Your heart-broken daughter told us how she felt
In a poem to you which made our hearts melt.
Our thoughts were with your family
As we all grieved as one.
They didn't lose a famous man,
But a husband, a father, a son.

Anne Smith,
Belfast

ANOTHER SOLDIER

Another soldier was killed, when will it end,
When will it stop, will they ever condescend
To hang up the guns, make bombing a thing of the past
Agree to a peace process, and make it last?
We will never please everyone, that goes without saying
We must stop shouting, and do some praying,
That young man in uniform was someone's son
Shot down in his prime before life's begun.
"He was only a soldier," you'll hear some folk say.
He was a person like us, now his life's thrown away.
Have you no conscience, you cowards with guns?
How many steps forward in all these years? NONE!
People have died, was it all in vain?
How long must we suffer killing and pain?
We could live together happily – let's give it a try,
To be friends with our neighbours instead of watching them die!

Anne Smith,
Belfast

AN ASIDE

The last thirty years of Belfast living
Hasn't left me bitter, or twisted,
But torn rather and less forgiving.

I was never that proud Prod.
I never saw a flag and thought
I must wave it for my Queen,
To me that's obscene.

I've never knelt before a man
As though he were God's own Priest
Or sat and gave thanks
At some sacrificial feast.

I never saw the contentious borders
Worth the dieing for,
except on board games.
(I was always red.)

Too many trapped minds,
Too many dead.

John L. Peshkin,
Belfast

DREAMS

Our dreams built with paper walls,
A deluge came, we watched them fall.
All our hopes lay strewn and broken,
When ancient voices within were woken.
"Arise, arise, don't bend the knee,
Be masters of your destiny."
From the diamond in the rough,
We built our dreams with stronger stuff.

Joseph McCullough,
Belfast

DAY OUT IN BELFAST

No one acknowledges each other's eyes
Or dares to listen to each other's sighs
As we sit on a bus going down the town
With all of our barriers firmly pinned down

The bus stops at one side
Then it stops on the other
Afraid of recognition
Our identities we smother
As both side's graffiti
Flies high on the day
Deeply offended
We just look away
The more abusive it becomes
As we leave the bus
Feeling so numb
The joy has gone out of a day round the town
On the way home, we will tread the same ground
Six of one, half a dozen of each other
Seems like we were all ducking for cover
Afraid of ourselves and a truth to discover
The sad reality is that this is our life
This thing we call Normality, so full of strife
It's not a rehearsal, for you and for me
Today, tomorrow, 'til eternity

Lily McWilliams,
Belfast

DOCKLAND CHILD

A landscape of family voices
Drifting in from the sea
An archive of dockers and sailors
Who once belonged to me
As I walked this barren dockland
Known as Sailortown of old
I find the dust has settled
On our legacy of gold
For all we dockland people
Who were so well moulded here
Are all still trapped in memories
Of our time called yesteryear
And the further we retreat from it
The more it calls us home
Our roots as we grow older
Are all we ever own
It's here we can find ourselves again
As we stand beside the sea
And hold our heads and proudly say
That dockland child was me

Lily McWilliams,
Belfast

OUT OF THE WINDOW

We'd look for the smoke and flames,
Guessing the exact spot.
Hear the explosion and argue over the whereabouts
Until the late-night news.

Now it's about seeing the swans
Swooping down to the Canal or a heron in flight.
Or we look out the window at the view,
Peaceful.

Sonia Craven Haddad,
Newry

AN EAST BELFAST CHILDHOOD

Ballymacarrett, East Belfast
Narrow streets – parallel and grey
Tiny pristine houses row on row
Many churches – little corner shops.

Looming, towering, two gigantic cranes
River of men flowing over the bridge
Striding, proudly purposeful
Belonging – almost tribal.

Two spires – one square, one pointed
St. Patrick's and opposite – St. Matthew's
Different styles, different faiths
Between them the broad and busy road.

Narrow streets long gone
The human river just a trickle now
Communities dispersed and in their place
Graffiti rules and the road is still broad.

Margaret Wilson,
Ballyclare

THE BIG MAN

I want to lie face down
And spread myself
Over Ulster.
I want him to stop meaning
For a while.

I want Ulster
To stop being
The fat-faced middle-aged white man
With the gritty, stubbly face;
The pint in one large red hand
And a growing child in the other.

Ulster was my father,
But he too was my mother.

Shirley-Anne McMillan,
Castlewellan

73

YOUR HOUSE

Child-faced and soaked
In cigarette fumes,
You sat and remembered
The big foxy dog
And the wee one that nipped you,
Your beautiful niece
And washing the floors of the students' union.

This road, a field of expectation,
Now a hot steaming tank of nostalgia.

It's where you watched Eastenders
And Alex Higgins' mammy
Cut your hair.

Shirley-Anne McMillan,
Castlewellan

74

TIME

Time will heal all wounds,
Or so people say.
Memories of loved ones
Never dacay.
A better tomorrow, no hate
And no pain,
In our Island of Beauty
Let love remain.

*(From a mother who has lost three sons
and whose anniversaries are in and around this time.
Written from the heart...)*

*Mrs. Bridget Logue,
Belfast*

TARGET

Silhouetted in the night
A target in a gunman's sight
Thunder – and a man lies dead
A pool of blood about his head
Comrades search but all in vain
A killer free to strike again.

Anon.

A LEAP OF FAITH

Look to the future
And not to the past
Build on peace and reconciliation
It's within your grasp.

In a country divided
By religion and creed
Just some understanding
Is all that we need.

A new tomorrow
A brighter sun
No hatred or pain
A better life for everyone.

Neely McGinley,
Co. Armagh

THOUGHTS ON
THE PAST AND THE FUTURE

It has been dark too long
I want a song
Put on your glad rags
Cut off the tags
Light the light
Let's party tonight.

In spite of all the troubles in thirty years or more
The people still have hearts of gold
And there's a welcome at any door.

We have cried rivers of tears
Told the world our hopes and fears
Our Winter time is past
It's Summer time at last.

When all our "Troubles" cease
And tears freely flow
The sun will come out in our hearts
And a better future we'll know.

A smile is only a frown
Turned upside down.

Maureen Bunting,
Belfast

BELFAST

Your face has changed,
the natural look replaced
with coloured cosmetic success
Your chest swells with pride
as you view new buildings
rising tall and grand
Dwarfing people as they stand
Wondering, looking in amazement
Where has old Belfast gone?
Searching for your green belt
hiding in the stone
Now the waistline is loose and wide
accepting all that comes
not always the best
Mighty arms stretch across the sky
to embrace the green hills
Alas, without the slopes once held
time to walk on and remember.

Hazel Wilson,
Dundonald

TWO FRIENDS

Belfast standing on the Lagan blue
Dwells deep within my heart 'tis true
Misty hills spread out their folds
like an emerald ring of gold.

The river weaves a gentle lane
twisting, turning, then on straight again
Passing through villages and towns
where people stop, listen to the river sounds
Lifting the heart with tones high and low.

Prosperity's wind has blown across the river's banks
where buildings grow in the night
Touching clouds in the morning light
Across the way music drifts from the new born dome
Different now from long ago.

Ask the Lagan how she feels.
unperturbed, no answer comes
Takes each new breeze in her flow
Her course is set, rippling waters take the blow.

The quiet river never rests, keeps moving on
at nature's behest
As evening falls the busy city is hushed to sleep
but the silent waters their watch must keep.

Hazel Wilson,
Dundonald

TAKE THE 'IRE' FROM IRELAND

The Mountains of Mourne weep down to the sea
Silent Valley is torn apart
The tears are real on the willow tree
There's rage in everyone's heart.

Banshees screech their wailing cry
It echoes in every glen
Who will be the next to die
From man's inhumanity to men?

Green grass is tainted red
No birds sing at dawn
A land fit only for the dead
All happiness is gone.

I will not say I'm Irish and proud
For I hang my head in shame
Stop it now! I cry out loud
Stop it in God's name!

Will the Lark one day return
To sing its joyful song?
Or will the hatred in our hearts still burn
And the killing go on and on.

Take the hate from this isle
Soothe away the pain
Make those Irish eyes beguile
Let happiness return again.

Take the 'Ire' from Ireland
The birds return to shore
Bring back joy to our land
Let Irish eyes smile once more.

Matthew Cosby,
Banbridge

WHAT'S IT ALL ABOUT?

What's it all about? I say
These past thirty years
Innocent people murdered
Bringing oh so many tears.

Can peace be totally found here?
A union through the land?
Of caring and loving each other
As God intended in His plan?

Can weapons be surrendered?
Agreements signed to be true?
Can Northern Ireland change now?
The next thirty years in view?

The answer isn't found here
It's found up above
Only God can change those evil ways
And turn those ways to love.

Allison Hamilton,
Belfast

THE SYLLABLES OF CHANGE

Every painted street mouth
Spoke of a deeper danger,
Clandestine Celts and Saxon shadows
Flickered and flashed, each to each a stranger.

Mouths now speaking the syllables of change
Across the contours of the city's face,
Easing the haunted echoes
From the once forbidden places.

Martin Magee,
Craigavon

CATCH A FALLING STAR

In the space of thirty summers
The word "peace" seemed an extinct form,
Such as the clouds of Neptune
Or the mountains of Mars.

But now like a falling star
Something rare enters our atmosphere.

Martin Magee,
Craigavon

REMEMBRANCE

Morning mist tumbles over headstones grey
Ivy clings to gravestones that once saw the light
Have they forgotten the light that shone there
Their loves remembered in the long grey mist.

And as you pass by some lettered muse
And sculptured deck
And winding mossy ways
And glance behind and glory at the dawn of day.

Henry Power,
Belfast

AURORA

Arise, Aurora, from thy slumbering bed
And waken all the earth with thy clarion call
And sun that raises with a shimmering glow
And sets her face on the earth below.

And all that flourish in the golden light
Raise up towards the dawn
And cast their mantles to the sun
And look forward to the day.

Henry Power,
Belfast

MY DEATH

I am not that old and I have seen it all
The murals on the brick walls
I have watched innocent people die
I have watched their loved ones cry and cry
I always said: It won't happen to me
But it did, as I came to see

I had it all, everything a girl dreams
A happy home and some one to love me
He went out with friends on a Saturday night
I thought he would be back, I was in for a fright
I heard bangs all night long
I thought they were fireworks
But I was wrong.

Then I heard the terrible news
Some one had been shot, some one I knew
I started worrying: Who could it be?
Then I got the phone call saying, Yes, Suzanne, it's Candy
I felt a hole develop in my heart
I thought it couldn't be – he said we would never be apart
I could feel my world crumble down around me
Everything I had had just been took
It was like reading someone's story from a book.

Now I knew what those families felt
All the hurt and pain that was dealt
Now all I have are memories of how things used to be
How we would walk hand in hand
Dreaming of that promised land.
I will never forget his warm eyes, his loving face
Him holding me in his warm embrace
All the love that we shared
No one will know how much he cared
Now I am without him I am so scared

A haunting whisper, a lonely cry
Deep down inside I constantly ask why
Why he was took so very young
I want to know who shot the gun
I have so many things I wish I had said
But now I can't because he is dead
I think of him every minute of the day
I wish that Saturday night I made him stay

I look at his picture every day
I close my eyes and often pray
To my Lord in heaven above
To look after the one I love
To keep him safe in his arms
Away from all of earth's harms
Tell him, even though we are apart,
I will love him forever with all my heart.

Suzanne Hyman,
Belfast

ANOTHER SOLUTION

Another solution, again, do we seek one?
Hidden in shadow, rhetoric and gun
Polarised by centuries,
We want they want
Government, peace, enough conflict
And political rant
Suffering, loss, pain
Of the silent, the articulate
A new millennium, a new start, again.

Harry Barry,
Dundonald

NEW AGREEMENT

Years of atrocity, a culture of blame,
and sad broken hearts. Other times too
when we stood in vigils, candles bright,
Yearning for peace and a future of light.

We negotiate now for a different lease
one the people can carry through.
human rights, justice, enduring peace.
Would anything less do for you?

Rhoda Watson,
Newtownabbey

THE TIMES THEY ARE A'CHANGING

It's nice to sit and think about
The many years gone by
Remembering mostly happy times
That come to you and I
But happy times for many folk
Within the Belfast scene
Were very rare, in fact I'd say
Were few and far between.
But happily our lives are changing
To things that are mostly good
Prosperity is knocking on our doors
As normally it should.
So let us grasp the chance that's come
And let's all pull our weight
So future generations here
Can have a first class fate.

Mr. F. Jackson,
Belfast

LAGAN WEIR

When I leave this city I will miss
The dirt-tinged warmth of sandstone and red brick,
The marching of meccano cranes,
And most of all
The starlings,
Painting their own wild murals on pale winter skies.

Carolyn Thompson,
Dundonald

BELFAST

Before every leftie faints all socialists taint
Every leftie for adhering, strictly to socialists
Leaning, for a socialist treats brothers as
Friends, even leftie fools a socialist forgives
All troubles brought even left's foolish liars
Sure all troubles brought even love every
Time sincerity arrives from leftie's educated browser.

Paddy Murphy,
Belfast

93

BELFAST

Born, bred and brought up
Educated, sure that was my bitter cup
Lavished with historical values
Forever lasting
Assessed in each generation
Sustained for each generation
Together we could go forward.

Paddy Murphy,
Belfast

MATERNITY WARD

In the common maternity ward
In sectarian Belfast
They forget it:
Praying one for another
And the unborn child.
Betty told me.

James Snoddy,
Belfast

CANCER CITY

This city has a cancer
Which unlike the dreaded kind
Festers not within the body
But is purely of the mind.
Please test yourself for infection
Do you hate some lowly one
Like a wandering, crying youngster
In a place called Ballymun
Can't you stand the pirouetting widow's only dance
On the orange day
Would you deny the piece of iced cake
And a cup of sugared tay
Brothers, sisters, comrades
This is not the Jesus way.

James Snoddy,
Belfast

LIGHT ON THE LAGAN

Blue light dances
on a timeless river.
At a place where salmon
once jumped over a ford,
as they answered a calling
back home to the hills.

Now they return
to clear waters of hope.
Avoiding dark rocks
that lie in the past.
Cautiously onwards
to a new peaceful light.

Michael Little,
Dundonald

END GAME?

Born on the cusp of thought
The peace has been hard fought

Is the price too high?
Sleeping dogs, should they lie?

Will tomorrow bring happier times?
Or will it be the same old chimes?

We will all have to wait and see,
What will be, will be.

Brendan F. Magee,
Belfast

COLOURS

Colours and Prods and colours and Papes
They're all different and still the same shapes
Distinguished by Seamus and Michael and Pat
From William and George and other names like that
There's green, white and gold
And red, white and blue
The Twelfth of July
And Ash Wednesday too
It's ingrained in our childhood
From the day that we walk
And gets more bitter from learning to talk
Then separate schools for Michael and me
Christian Brothers for him and Model for me
I've fallen in love with Briget McCann:
– Shit!

John McKittrick,
Hillsborough

HEADING BACK

I've had a mind to go again
Back home to my home town
Among the folk I love so well
With whom I wish to dwell

I've played a Scot for fifteen year
And drank her whisky dry
But it's back again to Ireland
And where I want to die

Among my ain folk as you say
But not expire just yet
I've just discovered poteen
And I'd like to wait a bit

To meet with friends at Ballymacnabb
Recall old times with townland lads
And in Armagh again proclaimed –
To be a city once again
To hold my brother's hand

John Ritchie,
Portstewart

A PRAYER FOR PEACE

Dear God, I feel so helpless,
When I look upon our land.
How men can kill each other,
I do not understand.

What can be gained by killing,
By taking some man's life –
By leaving sad and desolate,
His children and his wife?

Dear God, the day of judgement
Is drawing very near.
How will they face their Maker,
Will they even shed a tear?

Are their hearts so full of hatred,
Unmoved by death and pain?
Is there no end to evil,
Must we witness death again?

Please stop this pain and killing,
And make this hatred cease.
Give men some common sense, Lord
And please, God … give us peace!

Mrs. Harriet Brown,
Newtownards

LIFE.

For work is work, and nothing but,
No matter where you go.
You still must sweat amid the muck,
And toil to get the gold.
And all the while the shining years
In pride and loveliness,
Are flowing past like dreams or mist,
Into a nothingness

And some go up, and some go down,
And some who never move,
But round and round perpetually,
In an eternal groove.
And all the while the golden hours
As shadows in the sun.
Fleet in the winds of time and pass,
Till all the hours are done.

W.H. Lunn,
Groomsport

IRELAND: A SURREALIST STUDY

One step forward,
Ten steps back,
Words loaded like bullets
Catch innocents in their cross fire.
Ireland's own tower of Babel
Spirals up and up and up,
While the Garden of Eden
Is reduced to a wasteland.

Political jugglers clad in every hue
Spin their theories and dogma
With precarious expertise,
While the anxious silent majority
Gather with baited breath
For one deadly mistake.

The peace is uneasy
Floating like a confused angel
Caught in Hell.
Dali himself would be pleased with us
In this maze of chaos,
Bordered by cathedrals of silence
The only sound the baying dogs of war.

A lifetime wave of bitterness
Still floods these shores.
While peace is cast adrift,
Guided only by incompetent sailors
Who all crave to be captain.

Joanna Braniff,
Belfast

CHANGING FACE

Life has dealt kindly
With the City's face;
Its brightened thoroughfares
Outsmart the past
Whose halting steps
Endeavour to keep pace
With the forward race
Of time.

Deep in my memory
There lies the image
Of that earlier, older face
The city wore,
When scribbled streets
Stretched greyly here and there,
And ancient buildings tottered,
Brick on brick,
Before the onslaught
Of the passing years.

Yet glass walls are cold
Compared to mellow stone,
Must the wisdom of the old
Be forever overthrown?
I see a hint of tears
Hung on a century-shrouded sill
And feel the sorrow
These old stones have known.

Betty McIlroy,
Bangor

EARLY TRANSPORT

Cable trams trundled like caravans
on ancient trade routes
to promised lands,
Bellevue, Ballyhackamore, Castlereagh.

Tramlines reposed in cobblestones
cold reptilean arteries
steel fused with wheel;
a trolley rolled on electricity wire
a driver controlling the power.

On slatted seats up circular stairs
from the half moon open top
a crow's nest vantage point
viewing labyrinthine streets
and people going anywhere.
The conductor, god in his arena,
tugging a bell for start or stop
the platform kept clear.

Ita McMichael,
Ballycastle

LEARN TO FORGIVE

Do not hold hatred in your heart
Where it can hurt and maim
And cause you many sorrows
More than you could ever name
But strive to find forgiveness
That's God's lesson from above
That we should fill our hearts with
Peaceful thoughts and joy and love
So try a little every day
If someone's caused you pain
To find forgiveness in your heart
And it won't be in vain
And soon you'll find a way
To shed the thoughts
That make you blue
And find the strength to carry on
And friendships that are true
For peace and true contentment
Will be found if you impart
The thoughts of true forgiveness
From the bottom of your heart

Sylvia Butcher,
Belfast

KERBSTONE

All his efforts were focused
On this rectangle of
Concrete,
As if his life depended on it.

The brush strokes would have
Done justice to the Sistine
Chapel,
So much concentration in each one;

And when this one was done
The next beckoned,
Only he would have to change
Brush and colour
and change again
All the way down the street,

Until the traffic lights halted him
At the main road.

Three colours repeated.
A tri-colour marking out
The limits, like
Dogs pissing on lamp posts
For others to sniff and be
Warned.

Each little estate
Carefully described in
White and two others,
The meat and two veg of
Sectarian malice.

George Sproule,
Belfast

THERE'S ANOTHER SIDE

There's another side
to this battered city
that, for decades, hid its light
under a bushel of bombs and bullets.
The new Belfast rises vigorously
like a truculent phoenix,
the ashes of history and past wrongs
scattered wide
by the freshening west winds.

Valerie Morrison,
Lisburn

BELFAST MOUNTAINS

Majestic mountains
Mysterious by night and day
What stories they could tell
People come and go but they remain
We may change but they stay the same.

Will we have peace this year or next?
God willing, we will.
The mountains keep their secrets
But hope springs eternal.

Margaret Millar,
Belfast

TWO LITTLE BOYS

In the summer of '69
Two little boys played all day
In a field by the end of their street
And every day was one big treat
They were Robin Hood and William Tell
They fished in a stream, climbed trees the way boys do
And thought this time would never end.

In August, "Troubles" came to this land of ours
Robin Hood and William Tell were kept indoors
Life will never be the same again
And after all what was gained?

They sneaked out one day when the shooting stopped
To turn the clock was their intention
A bullet took young William Tell
When they had not gone very far.

He died for his country, people said
He died because people hated – that was all
And after all what was gained?

Margaret Millar,
Belfast

THE VOTER'S PLEA

If only we could make you see
The politicians here, I mean.
That forward if you choose to go
Bright futures for us all might grow.

Why backwards must you always look?
Old rivalries and fears to stoke.
Peace and goodwill. It's all we want.
Come on, blind sods. Wake up Stormont.

Maureen R. Cunningham,
Lisburn

FLYOVER

A big concrete flyover runs along what used to be your street
The planners called it progress, other voices spoke of lies and deceit.
The people and those old streets are now a place apart
But then the real Sailortown lies within the heart.

Gerry Gallagher, Secretary,
Sailortown Cultural and Historical Society

THE BEST WE COULD

My city in which I live,
Builds both future and past,
From Titanic to Waterfront
And now some peace at last!
Children are our future,
So let's build one that's good
Without war, then we'll say:
"We did the best we could."

Chris McCrory
Belfast

HERE AND NOW

Our land is in debate over state,
our future unsure, yet we stay,
are we worried it might be late
to change our minds or try to pray?
they argue back and forth, to and fro,
With our lives bound in their clumsy hands,
hope is only left for average Joe,
'cause who knows where one another stands?
It seems everyday I see their faces,
all their words heard through my ears,
while each in individual places,
we all know it will end in tears.
Voting-time again in this land of ours,
let's decide who deserves the powers.

Chris McCrory,
Belfast

WE WISH

Wreckage and ruin.
The fabric of people's lives.
Mangled bodies and minds;
the aftermath of bombs.
Sorrow and loss.
Have goals been achieved
to justify the heartbreak?

Let us fervently hope
that in times yet to come
each person will realise
the futility of destruction
and pull together, not apart.

Olivia Butler,
Belfast

AND NOW

Shattered glass, shattered lives
A woman cries.
Bomb and bullet echo out
a warning shout.
Mangled cars, burnt-out bars;
Let peace be ours!

Happy lives
our city thrives.
For this we strive
In times to come
let not our streets be overrun
by men with guns.

Olivia Butler,
Belfast

116

O HOW I LOVE BELFAST

As a child it was such a huge city
The trams along the streets
When I went to bed the noise in the streets
Kept me awake. But it was great.

Then I got older, I walked to work down
Duncairn Gardens, the little ladies washing their
Door steps, cleaning the windows. They
Always had a cheerful word.

No vandalism in those days, no broken windows,
Boarded up doors or graffiti on the walls.

What a change today –
Cars everywhere, buses coming in threes
No ladies cleaning
Lots of rubbish everywhere. Buildings boarded
Up. What a mess!
But I love Belfast!

Now we have beautiful buildings, huge office
Blocks and security men. I can shop 'til I drop
Lovely restaurants. Lots of people
How I shall cherish my memories forever.

E. Vance,
Lisburn

RELEASING

Wailing Bombs
Faceless Bullets
Petrifying Flesh.

Wiring Walls
Defeating Drums
Wrapped in flapping Mesh.

Swollen Salmon
Torquing Weirs
Oceans inching Earth.

Joe Ruane,
Armagh

WALKING BOTANIC

I walk Botanic
my arms heavy with shopping
hungry to be home.

Quiet in their plea
refugees sell Big Issues
aching for their own.

"Sorry, I have one,"
I say, avoiding their eyes
as I pass them by.

Katherine Martin

119

ADVANCE

Trainor's is gone – a black taxi
ran through the middle of the kitchen
Broad expanse of communication and
not of intellectual cognition
The ghosts of brick and glass
gaze towards the Hatchet Field
of the Black Mountain
What guillotine have they used
to sever belly from mouth
intelligence from relationships
law from justice
belonging from community spirit
And now they speak of education
as the way forward

Hugh G. Rice,
Ballycastle

120

A PLACE APART?

This is not a place apart,
Unique in its own ways,
Breath-taking in location,
Or inspired by its virtues.
People come and go,
Whilst others stay away
Fearing the place disagreeable.
Preachers preach no louder,
And lovers love no deeper.
Our loss is no greater;
Our wisdom no surer;
Our will remains in contrast.
This is home – This is Belfast.

John Peshkin

THE WALK …

(In Ligoniel there was a grave of the dog
that supposedly killed the last wolf in Wolf Hill.
We used to go walks to it when we were kids.)

There is no decay
Just over aggressive
Nature in the way.
This mucky mysterious place
Where once poor Jack lay.
The copse is swamped
And nettles
Win the day
In this dank place
Where once poor Jack lay.
My heart is stung
Not by thorn or nettle
Or the lack of sun.
But by my daughter's voice
Unconcerned.
"They dug him up
And threw his bones away.
There is no grave now
No place for Jack to lay.

Geraldine Reid

WHAT DAYS DO YOU LOVE THE BEST?

What days do you love the best?
Special time pockets you caress,
Loaded moments when the heart felt,
Burning glances that made you melt
Inside time, making days that can chime
Forever when everything else is in a mess.

What days do you love the best?

Hold on to them like the sea holds
Its waves, glide high for a short while
For they will break and die, swim on with
Abandon and you won't have to imagine for
They form like wine, lifting you to the rush of the sublime.

What days do you love the best?

Hold on to them like the earth holds
The rain, let them grow and flower
For they will wither and lose their power, wrap yourself
In their fragrance and you won't have to
Dance alone for they bloom like romance, giving you another chance.

What days do you love, the best?

Hold on to them like the mountains hold
The skies, breathe now in heaven's highs
For they get too cold for they are as old
As the earth's first sighs, listen to their tune
As they sing to the moon for you can't sleep in passion's tomb.

What days do you love the best?

Alan Crawford,
Belfast

123

IT IS BELFAST

I climbed to the top of Cavehill.
The city was lazy in a haze of fog.
The lights glistened like anchored ships.
The city is no longer divided by a
colour scheme of political paint.
The media reflects this grotesque image,
it blinkers our eyes with familiar, dead mirrors.
Beneath this tribal shroud lies a human city.
It is not choked with division
but thrives on diversity.
Shops are alive with characters,
not caricatures,
weather descriptions, comic wordplay,
the language of health, a lustful wink
and the unspoken appreciation between
the sexes.
It is this peculiar normality,
It is this contradiction in terms
that is the secret to Belfast's enduring charm
I can hear the cynics sharpening their tongues.
It is only to offer examples of distrust and hatred
but there is human warmth below the fog.
It is like the city's lights,
It is all around us.
It is Belfast.

Alan Crawford,
Belfast

THE HOUSE

Crouched beneath the cranes,
This house has watched shipyard workers
come home under their winking lights,
To a community bounded by culture – and
kerbstones.

Narrow, dark, terraced.
During the storms it waited like its cousins
across the city,
Cramped rooms offering refuge, but no
escape.

But three quarters of a century later there's
been a transformation.
Walls ripped down, blinds opened to let the
light in.
When I blow in – an English woman who
ticked the 'no religion' box,
I too look up to the cranes.
But alongside them on the horizon, the neon
of the peace dividend glows,
Guiding me home – and lighting the way to
the future.

Julia Paul
Belfast

REDUNDANT

Rusting gantries dangle limp like withered limbs.
Flat eyed men with heavy boots and burnt out dreams
Drag their cares behind with stifled screams
Down to the pub.
Then stagger home, anaesthetised with spirits raw,
Loath to face the day again, recriminations pain
Stuck in their craw

Fred McIlmoyle,
Bangor

HOPE

Yet, still we strive to keep hope's spark alive,
And see our dreams reborn in children's eyes.
A human theme, transcending trivial vanity.
To lose this dream, the ultimate profanity!

Fred McIlmoyle,
Bangor

NO ANAHORISH

I have no Anahorish,
I have no 'vowel-meadow'
To connect me to the past.

I know only the cool roughness of red brick
And the heavy surge of crowded streets.

Give me this new city of blue light,
I'll make my connections with it.

Michael McConkey,
BELB

LAST NIGHT I MET WITH CHRIST

Last night
I met with Christ
In Botanic Gardens

We sat
Side by side
Beneath the cherry blossom

And as each blossom fell, so did one tear.

Michael McConkey,
BELB

VOICES IN JAGGED WHITE

Voices in jagged white
a gull-yell in the clouds
a walk on the M 1
lifting off early tarmac
lit black with the setting sun

the fading light is busy
with strange blue; that time
for what quickly happens
before dark

lights coming on in the city
look quickly; imagine it
there; strange blue
that time for busily fading
is in the air

The cello sound of the road in summer
The thrumming of the sun on dry slate
The twang of a butterfly in the yard
Waiting for the lightness of music to return
A note in the air of possibility

The dazed clump of the winter road
Jitters eternity out of its sleep
And brings it down to pavement
We are sliding out of our skins
With the joy of what we don't know
Except that it is cold!

Una Woods
Belfast

130

COMING WORDS

The blunt of chimney
all is left of it against the dim-sunk day
say hurray
the time and place is right

stop still
a language is about to be committed
forgive it its trespasses

row-stacked upward towards the Springfield dam
say it
chimney-condemned space for its coming words
stark-still dusk behind

all the road falls victim
a hung jury the only air

is that it frail-glimmered on the Black mountain
then the act goes on
once committed on

A sharp gust of shadow shook the puddle
Black water widened like glass
sky at night
A face turned once the other way
A flight of stairs up to a landing
devoid of day
light from a street-lamp
broke into the tumbling shadow

Get away

Una Woods
Belfast

THE FUTURE IS LATE TONIGHT

The future is late tonight
the particular bang of a front door
The night is angry with the day
the white howl of a dog at midnight
The void is shaken in its space
the grip of rubber soles in a hall
The trees are shooting at the stars
the fire of branch on a lamp-lit blind

The child is awake and staring
the future is here tonight

Una Woods,
Belfast

THE TIME OF OUR LIVES

You were the
Minutes that made
Up the hours
The days the
Months the years
Of our lives.
From those who
Will always remember –
A time we
Will never forget.

Margaret Madden,
Belfast

HEAT

Unprejudiced light showers everyone,
developing negative and positive photographs
that flicker across the eye.

Nothing is ever black or white,
clenched fists and bloody palms
mop the brow.

Exposure to a different climate,
tolerance glistening
Ulster after the rain.

Iain C. Webb,
Newtownabbey

BELFAST

A child cradled in hatred.
            Snatched
from the womb of St. Patrick.
The child plays
            see
                    saw
with those who forsook God.

Belfast emerged from her chrysalis,
vibrant, red for the occasion.
Swirling, clicking
life's castanets.
Innocence stolen.

Now the sophisticated golden girl,
dancing to her own tune.
Cultural diversity her flimsy dress
            but
            still
        no resolution,
        no solution.

One day arthritic hands will entwine,
ignoring the pain from ancient wounds.
Tears will be released from failing eyes,
which shall strain to see the differences
that stole sons and daughters.
Ancient invocations are to be chanted–

    Christ within
    Christ around.

Wilma Kenny,
Belfast

135

HOPE

Scarcely a chink of light shone through;
And, yet, determined to survive,
She drew strength from every sinew
As if to keep all hope alive.
Patience strove with perseverance
To counter time that would delay
Her pilgrimage of endurance
Through the shadows to light of day.
Having fought through the cracked concrete,
She then outstretched her tongue-like leaves,
And there close by the quiet streets,
Pale yellow petals gently breathed.
Journey over, her battle won,
A wild primrose embraced the sun.

Robert Corrigan,
Portrush

WISE WORDS

You can't eat flags for breakfast.
That's what my mother always said.
And marching men; a month of Sundays,
never brought home brass nor bread.
Countries fought and died for:
never clothed; nor infants fed.
And anthem songs from dusk till dawn
could never stem the tears since shed.

Michael Mulholland,
Belfast

137

RECONSTRUCTION

Let's bury all our hatchets
Cremate the hate the hurt and harm
Let's resurrect our self-respect
Build our own tomorrow
Together arm in arm

Let's tear down all the barbed wire
and barricades inside our heads
Let forbearance be our bricks and mortar
Our future affirmation
To our children and our dead

Michael Mulholland,
Belfast

BELFAST

I am proud	humble
I am loud	soft spoken
I am bigoted	open minded
I am wounded	healing

I am a mass of contradiction
I am Belfast.

I am love to the stranger
Angry at my neighbour
I am building and investment
A thundering God and New Testament.

I am diversity of opinion
I am proud of this dominion
I am land to love and cherish
I am Northern Irish
I am Belfast.

Ann Cassidy,
Belfast

IN THIS PLACE

In this place you will know
a warmth to melt the granite spirit
speak to me of no tokenism
this is my home – I love it so.

Through sullied streets
it has remained where darkness
prevailed – in the tarnished towns
beauty and beast meet.

As I journey through life far and near
I will hear it whispering to my soul
and my heart will in unity confirm
there's no place like here.

Carolyn Hall,
Belfast

LIFE'S JOURNEY

As we live our life from day to day,
It is just once, we pass this way,
To other's compassion we should show
Then we will reap, just what we sow.

Respect and love, to others give,
Will then determine how we live,
This rule of life, lived day by day,
You just get back, what you give away.

So on this earth, time passes by,
To help all others we should try
To live our life, as best we can,
And always help our fellow man.

Mr. F. Bunting,
Newtownabbey

THE AGEING PROCESS

When in my youth
So full of zest
Now all I do
Is sit and rest.
My bones grow thin
My hair falls out
Yes that is what
Life's all about.
My eyes are dim
It's hard to see
Glasses for me
It has to be.
My ears are bad
And it's hard to hear
It's a hearing aid
For me I fear.
My legs get tired
When I walk about
If I walk upstairs
Then my puff runs out.
It's the ageing process
So we are told
But the fact remains
We're just growing old.

Mr. F. Bunting,
Newtownabbey

OCEAN BRIDGE

'To build a bridge over an ocean
would be a worthwhile but veritable task.'
'Would it be quicker to fly?' I heard someone ask.
'Perhaps,' I replied, 'I see what you mean,
but hurricanes can appear just whenever it seems,
But a bridge built on foundations sturdy and deep,
Can last throughout ages without falling in a heap.'
Then someone piped up with a smile and a gloat,
'Surely it would be easier to get on a boat.'
'Alas,' said I, 'there's troubled waters,
Not to mention cold drink, remember that Belfast boat
That God Himself could not sink.'
'No, a bridge can give passage from one way to the next,
A boat would be insufferably slow in betwixt.'
Then a sinister voice called out from the next room,
'And what if someone blows up the bridge at high noon?'
I pondered in fear at this question insane...
But better a bridge than a boat or a plane,
The latter of which would n'er be seen again.

Andrew D. Glover,
Belfast

CHILDSPLAY

I remember back in my day
When life was full of hope
Children playing, skipping
Mummies held the rope
Daddies joined in Rounders
Cycled up and down the street
A game of good old hopscotch
Was very hard to beat
Such joy we had as youngsters
Playing haunts on summer nights
Two-ball was a daily game
And one, two, three, red-lights!
It took little to amuse us then
Oh how we loved to play
Pity kids are missing out
The youngsters of today
If they saw kids playing old games
They'd probably stop and stare
But give me old games everytime
'cause nothing could compare!

Yvonne Henry,
Belfast

FACE UP

1.

Face up to your convictions
Let your voice follow heart
You know you can do it if you try
Put aside all temptations
Let your mind search for truth
If you don't, you'll be sorry when you die.

2.

Some think it necessary to use violence for peace,
Every day people would argue and say: Please,
Stop and think before we hurt someone,
Sit around a table and plan.
Our future is not the bullet or the bomb,
Or the amount of bodies we put in a tomb,
Speak to our enemies, then decide,
If we're fighting for peace, victory or pride.

3.

If we had peace 30 years ago
Think where we could be now
That would be hard to imagine.

When we get peace, sooner or later
What a bright future it will be for everyone,
That would be easy to imagine.

Jay Boreen,
Belfast

PEOPLE OF WAR

There's a dying breed of people,
For whom I do adore,
And yet I wouldn't be sad,
When they finally are no more.
For the very thing that made them,
My loyal, trusty friends,
Was the trouble of their homeland,
So many painful ends.
It pulled them all together,
Yet tore two sides apart,
So many people crying,
With that a change of heart.
To look into the future,
And see the peace, both sides,
To understand tradition,
Equality and pride.

Jane Grace,
Belfast

146

A LITTLE REMINDER

Peace at last,
What a relief,
I forget the trouble,
And the grief,
But sometimes a little,
Reminder of
When the helicopter
Flies direct, above.

Jane Grace,
Belfast

JUST LIKE ME

Across the border
I do see
A human being
Just like me
Not tarred with
Everlasting hate
Just frightened they'll
Become "Free State".

Jane Grace,
Belfast

JOURNEY

We are all into this journey
Although on different paths
We were born to different colours
Religions, social class
We have many different talents
Thank God, not all the same
Making us unique
In life, to fail or gain.
A slave to our emotions
And narrow-minded views
For all of this uniqueness
A war divided in two.
Our hate released with anger
Our fear still trapped inside
Fearing of a change we want
Or want denied.

Jane Grace,
Belfast

PROZAC TANTO QUID

Sweet little pill
Take every day
You're not really ill
Keep the Black Dog away
Life without peace
Bitter to swallow
Belfast today
Existence is hollow
Sweet little pill
Take every day
You're not really ill
Keep the Black Dog away

One half is cream
Green is the other
One man is Orange
Green is his brother

Sweet little pill
Take every day
You're not really ill
Keep the Black Dog away
Sweet little pill
All over our city
Take every day
Replacement for pity
Sweet little pill
Take every day
You're not really ill
Keep the Black Dog away

Joyce Finlay,
Martin Centre